MW01046351

With love to Reuben and Luca.
"Reading unlocks the world, the world is yours!"

Special thanks to Andrea Fourie, a wonderful friend
and specialist Speech Language Pathologist, for your patience,
love and keeping us true to developmental principles.

© Publication: LAPA Publishers (Pty) Ltd
380 Bosman Street, Pretoria
Tel. 012 401 0700
E-mail: lapa@lapa.co.za
© Text: Jose Palmer and Reinette Lombard 2019
© Illustrations: Zinelda McDonald 2019

Set in 35 pt on 38.4 pt Edu-Aid Gr 1 Solid
Layout and design: Full Circle
Printed by ABC Press

First edition 2019

ISBN 978 0 7993 9703 1

Learn to read

Level 1: Book 5

Tippie and Mum

LAPA Publishers
www.lapa.co.za

This is Tippie.

This is Mum.

Tippie and Mum want to have fun.

This is a bus.

Tippie and Mum are on the bus.

Going on a bus is fun.

Tippie and Mum are going
to see Gran.

This is Tippie's Gran.

Gran is Mum's mum.

Gran lives in a hut.
Gran lives in a mud hut.

Tippie runs to Gran.

Tippie jumps up, up, up.

Tippie gives Gran a big,
big, big hug.

It is fun to see Mum's
mum.

Activities

Word list	
Mum	Mum
fun	fun
bus	bus
hut	hut
mud	mud
run	run
hug	hug
up	up
Tippie	Tippie
Gran	Gran

Connect the rhyming words

mud   dug

fun   rut

hut   dud

hug   sun

Scramble the letters to build words

n u f	
s u b	
t u h	
g h u	
d u m	

Circle the pictures that have a short -u- vowel

Comprehension

1. What do Tippie and Mum want to do?

2. Where are they going?

3. Who is Mum's mum?

4. What does Tippie give Gran?

5. Where does Gran live?

Match the word to the picture

hut

mud

run

fun

hug

bus

Mum

Word search

Find the words and colour the blocks

mum   fun   bus   hut

run   up   hug   sun

mud   nut

n	u	t	a	b	c	d	h	f
g	h	i	b	u	s	j	u	k
r	r	q	p	o	n	m	t	l
u	s	u	p	t	u	v	w	x
n	y	x	a	b	c	s	u	n
d	e	f	f	u	n	g	h	i
j	k	l	m	n	o	m	p	q
h	u	g	r	s	t	u	v	w
x	y	z	q	s	r	m	b	m
r	t	m	u	d	e	d	v	n

Complete the sentences

Tippie and _____ want
to have _____.

This is a _____.

Going on a bus is _____.

Tippie and Mum are going
to see _____ mum.

Gran lives in a _____.

Tippie _____ up.